MOON MAN

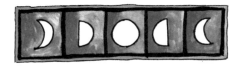

MOON MAN

TOMI UNGERER

HARPER & ROW, PUBLISHERS   NEW YORK

MOON MAN

By arrangement with Diogenes Verlag, Zürich, for Harper & Row, Publishers, Incorporated,
1967. This work is protected under the International Copyright Union. All rights reserved.
For information address Harper & Row, Publishers, Incorporated, 49 East 33rd Street,
New York, N. Y. 10016.

Printed in the Netherlands.

Library of Congress Catalog Card Number: 66-12135

On clear, starry nights the Moon Man can be seen curled up
in his shimmering seat in space.

Every night from his drifting sphere the Moon Man was filled with envy
as he watched the Earth people dance.

"If only once I could join the fun," he thought.
"Life up here is such a bore."

One night a shooting star flashed by.

The Moon Man leaped just in time to catch the fiery tail of the comet.

The night creatures of the woods fled in terror

at the loud crash of the fallen star.

The noise brought hundreds of people from a nearby town.

Soldiers sped to defend the earth. Firemen hastened to quench
the flaming light.

*The ice cream man hurried to set up his stand for the spectators.

When they reached the site of the crash, no one could decide

what the pale, soft creature lying in the crater could be.

15

Government officials were alerted.
Statesmen, scientists, and generals panicked.

They called the mysterious visitor an invader.

The Moon Man was thrown in jail while a special court conducted
a criminal investigation.

Poor Moon Man...his hopes of dancing among the gay crowds
and bright lanterns were crushed.

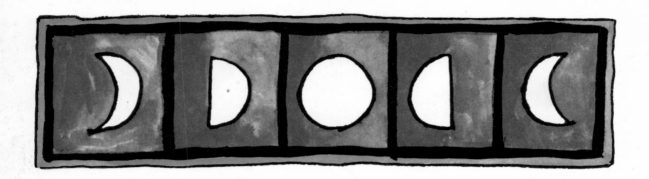

One night as the Moon Man sat wondering why he was so cruelly treated
he noticed that his left side had faded.
"Why, I must be in my third quarter," he thought happily.

Every night as the moon grew thinner and thinner so did the Moon Man,
until at last he was able to squeeze through the bars of his window.

When the head of the armed forces paid a visit to inspect the weird captive,

he found the cell empty. The general was furious.

Days later, as the moon reappeared in its first quarter,
a quarter of the Moon Man came back.
Two weeks later he had reached his full size again.

Delighted with his freedom, he wandered about discovering
the sweet-smelling flowers, the marvelous birds, and butterflies.

He came upon a garden party where people in gorgeous costumes
were dancing.

"Look! Someone has come as the man in the moon," a lady cried.
The Moon Man danced blissfully for hours.

Alas, a grumpy neighbor complained of the late music to the police.
Scared by the sight of the guns and uniforms,

the Moon Man dashed off to the nearby woods.
But he was spotted by the policemen, and a wild chase began.

Swiftly outracing the police, the Moon Man shot across the countryside.

In a lonely place he came upon an ancient castle.

There he was welcomed by a long-forgotten scientist,
Doktor Bunsen van der Dunkel.

For centuries he had been perfecting a spacecraft to reach the moon.

Now finished, the intricate machine rested on its launching pad
on a castle turret. Doktor van der Dunkel had grown too old and too fat
to fit into the capsule. He asked his guest to be his first passenger.

The Moon Man, who had realized that he could never live peacefully on this planet, agreed to go.

Doktor van der Dunkel decided to wait for the moon to enter
its third quarter. "By then the Moon Man will have grown
small enough to fit into the capsule," he thought. A few nights
later, the Moon Man took leave of his benefactor.
With tears in their eyes they bade each other farewell.

Then the Moon Man blasted off with a roar of rockets.

99 *Having succeeded in the launching of his spacecraft,*
Doktor van der Dunkel at last received the recognition
he had so long deserved.

He was elected chairman of an important · · · · · · · ·

Having satisfied his curiosity, the Moon Man never returned to earth
and remained ever after curled up in his shimmering seat in space.

DATE DUE

5 9DEC 14 '93		
1 2 JAN 17 '94		
2 MAR 28 '94		
1 1 APR 22 '94		
5 OOCT 27 '94		
1 2 NOV 14 '94		
7 2 FEB 6 '95		
1 0 APR 14 '95		
1 1 MAY 19 '95		

DEMCO 38-297